The Giant Roc

and other stories

Miles Kelly

First published in 2011 by Miles Kelly Publishing Ltd
Harding's Barn, Bardfield End Green, Thaxted, Essex, CM6 3PX, UK

Copyright © Miles Kelly Publishing Ltd 2011

This edition printed 2013

2 4 6 8 10 9 7 5 3

Publishing Director Belinda Gallagher
Creative Director Jo Cowan
Editor Amanda Askew
Senior Designer Joe Jones
Production Manager Elizabeth Collins
Reprographics Anthony Cambray, Stephan Davis, Lorraine King, Jennifer Hunt
Assets Lorraine King

ISBN 978-1-84810-502-7

Printed in China

· British Library Cataloguing-in-Publication Data
A catalogue record for this book is available from the British Library

ACKNOWLEDGEMENTS
Artworks are from the Miles Kelly Artwork Bank

Cover artwork by Rupert van Wyck (Beehive Illustration)

Every effort has been made to acknowledge the source and copyright holder of each picture.
Miles Kelly Publishing apologises for any unintentional errors or omissions.

Made with paper from a sustainable forest

www.mileskelly.net
info@mileskelly.net
www.factsforprojects.com

Contents

The Giant Roc

From *The Second Voyage of Sinbad the Sailor*

I DESIGNED, AFTER MY FIRST VOYAGE, to spend the rest of my days at Bagdad, but it was not long ere I grew weary of an indolent life, and I put to sea a second time, with merchants of known probity. We embarked on board a good ship, and, after recommending ourselves to God, set sail. We traded from island to island, and exchanged commodities with great profit. One day we landed on an island covered with several sorts of fruit trees, but we could see neither man nor animal. We walked in the meadows, along the streams that watered them. While some diverted themselves with gathering flowers, and others fruits, I took my wine and provisions, and sat down near a stream betwixt two high trees, which formed a thick shade. I made a good meal, and afterward fell asleep. I cannot tell how long I slept, but when I awoke the ship was gone.

In this sad condition I was ready to die with grief. I cried out in agony, beat my head and breast, and threw myself upon the ground, where I lay some time in despair. I upbraided myself a hundred times for not being content with the produce of my first voyage, that might have sufficed me all my life. But all this was in vain, and my repentance came too late. At last I resigned myself to the will of God. Not knowing what to do, I climbed to the top of a lofty tree, from whence I looked about on all sides, to see if I could discover anything that could give me hope. When I gazed toward the sea I could see nothing but sky and water; but looking over the land, I beheld something white; and coming down, I took what provision I had left and went toward it, the distance being so great that I could not distinguish what it was.

As I approached, I thought it to be a white dome, of a prodigious height and extent; and when I came up to it, I touched it, and found it to be very smooth. I went round to see if it was open on any side, but saw it was not, and that there was no climbing up to the top, as it was so smooth. It was at least fifty paces round.

By this time the sun was about to set, and all of a sudden the sky became as dark as if it had been covered with a thick cloud. I was much astonished at this sudden darkness, but much more when I found it was occasioned by a bird of a monstrous size, that came flying toward me. I remembered that I had often heard mariners speak of a miraculous bird called the roc, and conceived that the great dome which I so much admired must be its egg. In short, the bird alighted, and sat over the egg. As I perceived her coming, I crept close to the egg, so that I had before me one of the legs of the bird, which was as big as the trunk of a tree. I tied myself strongly to it with my turban, in hopes that the roc next morning would carry me with her out of this desert island. After having passed the night in this condition, the bird flew away as soon as it was daylight, and carried me so high that I could not discern the earth; she afterward descended with so much rapidity that I lost my senses. But when I found myself on the ground, I speedily untied the knot, and had scarcely done so, when the roc, having taken up a serpent of a monstrous length in her bill, flew away.

The spot where it left me was encompassed on all sides by mountains, that seemed to reach above the clouds, and so steep that there was no possibility of getting out of the valley. This was a new perplexity; so that when I compared this place with the desert island from which the roc had brought me, I found that I had gained nothing by the change.

As I walked through this valley, I perceived it was strewn with diamonds, some of which were of surprising bigness. I took pleasure in looking upon them; but shortly I saw at a distance such objects as greatly diminished my satisfaction, and which I could not view without terror, namely, a great number of serpents, so monstrous that the least of them was capable of swallowing an elephant. They retired in the daytime to their dens, where they hid themselves from the roc, their enemy, and came out only in the night.

I spent the day in walking about in the valley, resting myself at times in such places as I thought most convenient. When night came on I went into a cave, where I thought I might repose in safety. I secured the entrance, which was low and narrow, with a great stone, to preserve me from the serpents; but not so far as to exclude the light. I supped on part of my provisions, but the serpents, which began hissing round me, put me into such extreme fear that I did not sleep. When day appeared the serpents retired, and I came out of the cave, trembling. I can justly say that I walked upon diamonds without feeling any inclination to touch them. At last I sat down, and notwithstanding my apprehensions, not having closed my eyes during the night, fell asleep, after having eaten a little more of my provisions. But I had scarcely shut my eyes when something that fell by me with a great noise awakened me. This was a large piece of raw meat; and at the same time I saw several others fall down from the rocks in different places.

I had always regarded as fabulous what I had heard sailors and others relate of the valley of diamonds, and of the stratagems employed by merchants to obtain jewels from thence; but now I found that they had stated nothing but the truth. For the fact is, that the merchants come to the neighbourhood of this valley, when the eagles have young ones, and throwing great joints of meat into the valley, the diamonds, upon whose points they fall, stick to them; the eagles, which are stronger in this country than anywhere else, pounce with great force upon those pieces of meat, and carry them to their nests on the precipices of the rocks to feed their young: the merchants at this time run to their nests, disturb and drive off the eagles by their shouts, and take away the diamonds that stick to the meat.

I perceived in this device the means of my deliverance.

Having collected together the largest diamonds I could find, and put them into the leather bag in which I used to carry my provisions, I took the largest of the pieces of meat, tied it close round me with the cloth of my turban, and then laid myself upon the ground, with my face downward, the bag of diamonds being made fast to my girdle.

I had scarcely placed myself in this posture when one of the eagles, having taken me up with the piece of meat to which I was fastened, carried me to his nest on the top of the mountain. The merchants immediately began their shouting to frighten the eagles; and when they had obliged them to quit their prey, one of them came to the nest where I was. He was much alarmed when he saw me; but recovering himself, instead of inquiring how I came thither, began to quarrel with me, and asked why I stole his goods.

"Do not be uneasy; I have diamonds enough for you and myself, more than all the other merchants together." I had scarcely done speaking, when the other merchants came crowding about us, much astonished to see me; but they were much more surprised when I told them my story.

They conducted me to their encampment; and there, having opened my bag, they were surprised at the largeness of my diamonds, and confessed that they had never seen any of such size and perfection. I prayed the merchant who owned the nest to which I had been carried (for every merchant had his own) to take as many for his share as he pleased. He contented himself with one, and that, too, the least of them.

The merchants had thrown their pieces of meat into the valley for several days; and each of them being satisfied with the diamonds that had fallen to his lot, we left the place the next morning, and travelled near high mountains.

I pass over many things peculiar to this island, lest I should weary you. Here I exchanged some of my diamonds for merchandise. From hence we went to other islands, and at last, having touched at several trading towns of the continent, we landed at Bussorah, from whence I proceeded to Bagdad. There I immediately gave large presents to the poor, and lived honorably upon the vast riches I had brought, and gained with so much fatigue.

The Three Heads of the Well

By Flora Annie Steel

ONCE UPON A TIME there reigned a king in Colchester who was valiant, strong, wise, and famous throughout the land as a good ruler. But in the midst of his glory his dear queen died, leaving him with a daughter to look after. This maiden was renowned for her beauty, kindness and grace.

Now strange things happen – the king of Colchester heard of a lady who had immense riches, and had a mind to marry her, although she was old, ugly, hook-nosed, and ill-tempered. Furthermore, she possessed a daughter as ugly as herself. None could give the reason why, but only a few weeks after the death of his dear queen, the king married her with great pomp and festivities. Now the first thing she did was to poison the king's mind against his daughter, of whom, the ugly queen and her ugly daughter were jealous.

Now when the young princess found that even her father had turned against her, she grew weary of court life, and longed to get away from it. So, one day, she went down on her knees, and begged and prayed for the king to give her some help, and let her go out into the world to seek her fortune. To this the king agreed, and the ugly queen only gave her a canvas bag of brown bread and hard cheese, with a bottle of small-beer.

Though this was but a pitiful dowry for a king's daughter, the princess was too proud to complain, so she took it and set off on her journey.

At last she came to a cave at the mouth of which, on a stone, sat an old, old man with a white beard.

"Good day, fair damsel," he said, "where are you going?"

"Reverend father," replied she, "I'm going to seek my fortune."

"And what have you a dowry, fair damsel," said he, "in your bag and bottle?"

"Bread and cheese and small-beer, father," said she, smiling. "Will it please you to partake of either?"

"With all my heart," said he, and when she pulled out her provisions he ate them nearly all. But once again she made no complaint.

Now when he had finished he gave her many thanks, and said, "For your beauty, and your kindness, and your grace, take this wand. There is a thick thorny hedge before you that seems impassable. But strike it thrice with this wand, saying each time, 'Please, hedge, let me through,' and it will open a pathway for you. Then, when you come to a well, sit down, do not be surprised at anything you may see, but, whatever you are asked to do, please do!"

So she went on her way. After a while she came to a high, thick thorny hedge, but when she struck it three times with the wand, saying, "Please, hedge, let me through," it opened a wide pathway for her. So she came to the well, on the brink of which she sat down, and no sooner had she done so, than a golden head without any body came up through the water, singing as it came:

"Wash me and comb me, lay me on a bank to dry
    Softly and prettily to watch the passers-by."

"Certainly," she said, pulling out her silver comb. Then, placing the head on her lap, she began to comb the golden hair. When she had combed it, she lifted the golden head softly, and laid it on a primrose bank to dry. No sooner had she done this than another golden head appeared, singing as it came:

"Wash me and comb me, lay me on a bank to dry
    Softly and prettily to watch the passers-by."

"Certainly," said she, and after combing the golden hair, placed the golden head softly on the primrose bank, beside the first one.

Then came a third head out of the well, and it said the same thing:

"Wash me and comb me, lay me on a bank to dry
    Softly and prettily to watch the passers-by."

"With all my heart," said she graciously, and after taking the head on her lap, and combing its golden hair with her silver comb, there were the three golden heads in a row on the primrose bank. She sat down to rest and cheerfully ate and drank the meagre portion of the brown bread, hard cheese, and small-beer that the old man had left to her, for, though she was a king's daughter, she was too proud to complain.

Then the first head spoke. "What shall we 'weird' for this damsel who has been so gracious? I 'weird' her to be so beautiful that she shall charm every one she meets."

"And I," said the second head, "'weird' her a voice that shall exceed the nightingale's in sweetness."

"And I," said the third head, "'weird' her to be so fortunate that she shall marry the greatest king alive."

"Thank you with all my heart," said she, "but don't you think I had better put you back in the well before I go on? Remember you are golden, and the passers-by might steal you."

To this they agreed, so she put them back. And when they had thanked her for her kind thought and said goodbye, she went on her journey.

Now she had not travelled far before she came to a forest where the king of the country was hunting with his nobles. The king caught sight of her, and drew up his horse, amazed at her beauty. He jumped from his horse and falling on his knee begged and prayed her to marry him without delay. And he begged and prayed so well that at last she consented.

So, they returned to his palace, where the wedding festivities took place with all possible pomp and merriment. Then, ordering out the royal chariot, the happy pair departed to pay the king of Colchester a bridal visit. You may imagine the surprise and delight with which, after so short an absence, the people of Colchester saw their beloved, beautiful, kind and gracious princess return in a chariot as the bride of the most powerful king in the world. The bells rang out, flags flew, drums beat, the people cheered, and all was gladness, save for the ugly queen and her ugly daughter, who were ready to burst with envy, for the despised maiden was now above them both, and went before them at every court ceremony.

So, after the visit was ended, and the young king and his bride had gone back to their own country to live happily ever after, the ugly, ill-natured princess said to her mother, the ugly queen:

"I also will go into the world and seek my fortune. If that drab of a girl with her mincing ways got so much, what may I not get?"

So her mother agreed, and furnished her forth with silken dresses and furs, and gave her as provisions sugar, almonds, and sweetmeats of every variety, besides a large flagon of Malaga wine. Altogether a right royal dowry fit for a princess.

Armed with her plentiful package the ugly princess set forth on her journey, following the same road as her stepsister. Thus she soon came upon the same old man with a white beard, who was seated on a stone by the mouth of a cave.

"Good day" said he. "Where are you going?"

"What's that to you, old man?" she said rudely.

"And what have you for a dowry in bag and bottle?" he asked quietly.

"Good things with which you shall not be troubled," she answered pertly.

"Will you not spare an old man something to eat?" he said.

Then she laughed. "Not a bite, not a sup, lest they should choke you, though that would be small matter to me," she replied, with a toss of her head.

"Then ill luck go with you," remarked the old man as he rose and went into the cave.

So she went on her way, and after a time came to the thick, thorny hedge, and seeing what she thought was a gap in it, she tried to pass through, but no sooner had she got well into the middle of the hedge than the thorns closed in around her so that she was all scratched and torn before she won her way. Thus, streaming with blood, she went on to the well, and seeing water, sat on the brink intending to cleanse herself. But just as she dipped her hands, up came a golden head singing as it came:

"Wash me and comb me, lay me on the bank to dry
Softly and prettily to watch the passers-by."

"A likely story," said she. "I'm going to wash myself, thank you very much." And with that she gave the head such a bang with her bottle that it bobbed below the water. But it came up again, and so did a second head, singing as it came:

"Wash me and comb me, lay me on the bank to dry
Softly and prettily to watch the passers-by."

"Not I," scoffed she. "I'm going to wash my hands

and face and have my dinner." So she gave the second head a cruel bang with the bottle, and both heads ducked down in the water.

But when they came up again all draggled and dripping, the third head came also, singing as it came:

"Wash me and comb me, lay me on the bank to dry
   Softly and prettily to watch the passers-by."

By this time the ugly princess had cleansed herself, and, seated on the primrose bank, had her mouth full of sugar and almonds.

"Not I," said she as well as she could. "I'm not a washerwoman nor a barber. So take that for your washing and combing."

And with that, she finished the wine, carelessly flung the empty bottle at the three heads floating in the well, and carried on greedily eating her sweets.

But this time the heads didn't duck. They looked at each other and said, "How shall we 'weird' this rude girl for her bad manners?"

"I 'weird' that to her ugliness shall be added blotches on her face," said the first head.

"And I 'weird' that she shall forever be hoarse as a crow and speak as if she had her mouth full," said the second head.

"And I 'weird' that she shall be glad to marry a cobbler," said the third head.

Then the three heads sank into the well and were no more seen, and the ugly princess went on her way. But, lo and behold! When she came to a town, the children ran from her ugly blotched face screaming with fright.

Now in the town there happened to be a cobbler who seeing the miserable, ugly princess in great distress craftily said that if she would take him for a husband he would undertake to cure her.

"Anything! Anything!" sobbed the princess.

So they were married, and the cobbler straightway set off with his bride to visit the king of Colchester. Instead of cheering, the people burst into guffaws at the cobbler in leather, and his wife in silks and satins.

As for the ugly queen, she was so enraged that she went mad with anger, and left the country. Whereupon the king, really pleased at getting rid of her so soon, gave the cobbler one hundred pounds and bade him go about his business with his ugly bride!

The Curse of Andvari's Ring

A Norse myth

IT OFTEN PLEASED ODIN, the chief of the gods, to disguise himself with a broad-brimmed hat and travelling cloak, and go wandering through Midgard to see all that was happening in the world of men. For one such journey, Odin was accompanied by his brother, Hoenir, and the troublemaker Loki. The three were strolling along, following the course of the river when they saw an otter basking in the sun, eating salmon. The quick and cunning Loki instantly snatched up a stone and threw it at the otter, aiming perfectly and knocking it dead. "Aha!" he cried, triumphantly. "Two prizes with a single shot – and just in time for lunch!"

It wasn't long before Loki was skinning the otter, while Hoenir built a fire and Odin roasted the salmon. Before the gods had tasted even a morsel of their meal, a very small, but very furious, man appeared from over a craggy ledge and strode towards them. As he approached, he drew his gleaming sword and brandished it threateningly. "I am Hreidmar, King of the Dwarves, and I demand vengeance!" he roared, purple-faced with rage.

The gods leapt to their feet at once in alarm. "Vengeance?" Hoenir protested, "but we have done nothing to offend you."

"Nothing!" spat the king. "Nothing! You call slaughtering one of my sons nothing!" And Hreidmar pointed to the otter skin dangling from Loki's hand.

The gods looked at each other in horror. They realized at once what had happened. Dwarves knew very strong magic and some of them could even change shape and take on animal form. The gods thought that Loki had killed an otter, but in fact it was a dwarf prince.

Two burly dwarves came running up behind Hreidmar, one clutching a stone axe and the other with a dagger.

"My remaining sons, Fafnir and Regin, will have justice!" Hreidmar thundered, as the men advanced.

"You will forfeit a life for the life you have taken!" one bellowed.

"Who will pay the price for murdering our brother?" the other raged, edging closer.

"Wait a moment!" cried Odin, thinking fast. "You will gain nothing from killing any of us. However, you will profit well if we pay you compensation instead. It is true that we have grievously wronged you. Now tell us, what is the price of making amends?"

Hreidmar lifted his hand, halting Fafnir and Regin in their tracks. The dwarves turned to each other and consulted for a minute or two. With a greedy smile, Hreidmar nodded. "So be it. You shall bring enough gold to fill the skin of the otter that was once my beloved son, and to cover it entirely. Choose one of you to go and fetch the gold. The other two must remain here as our hostages." Hreidmar grinned as the otter skin grew larger and larger before their very eyes.

"I will go," Loki volunteered, relishing the chance to outdo the tricksters. "I know where there is a trove of treasure so large, it should easily satisfy your needs – although it will take all the cunning I possess if I am to lay my hands on it." Without delay, he sped off, leaving Odin and Hoenir at the mercy of the dwarves.

Loki knew that for his plan to work, he would have to beg for the help of the giants – sworn enemies of the gods. He needed a favour from Ran, the cold-hearted wife of the giant who ruled the sea. Loki wanted to borrow Ran's enchanted fishing net, which she used to catch shipwrecked sailors and drown them in the deeps. Fortunately, only because Loki was half-giant, Ran grudgingly agreed.

Next, Loki journeyed to a place where a mighty waterfall thundered over a towering cliff into a plunging pool – the home of another dwarf, Andvari. Although Loki had had enough dealings with dwarves to last him a lifetime, he knew of no one else to turn to. Andvari was believed to have a secret treasure trove, as large as the highest mountain. Keeping his fingers crossed, Loki just hoped that the rumours were true…

Loki settled himself by the side of the pool and used his power to blend his body into the landscape. An unseeing mouse ran over his foot. An unnoticing butterfly came and settled on his nose. But not once did Loki stir. He just sat… and watched… and waited. At last he saw a trout that was bigger and shinier than all the other fish. Swifter than a darting kingfisher, he cast Ran's net, ensnared the trout, and drew it spluttering and flapping onto the bank. Grabbing it, Loki squeezed as hard as he could, until suddenly the trout changed shape – into the dwarf, Andvari!

"Stop! Stop!" Andvari gasped. "Tell me what you want and stop squashing the life out of me!"

Easing his grip a little, Loki made his demands. The dwarf was outraged, but imprisoned in Loki's clutches, he had no choice. Fuming, he directed Loki up a secret pathway behind the waterfall, to a cave that was filled from floor to ceiling with an incredible sight – gold. Gold cups, gold crowns, gold coins, gold necklaces, gold rings, gold bracelets, gold earrings, gold weapons, gold belts, gold brooches – a million and one golden objects glistened and gleamed in the darkness. With his eyes wide, Loki said "I need it all – and I mean all."

Sulking, Andvari helped Loki to pack up all his treasure, until there was no sign that the gold had ever been there. "That's it," Andvari sighed, mournfully. "I've given you everything."

"Not quite everything," corrected Loki, taking a ring from Andvari's little finger. "Please, I've given you all the gold I have. Allow me to keep this one small ring."

"I told you," Loki insisted firmly, "I need it all."

"Then have it!" cried the devastated dwarf. "And may a curse of sorrow be on it for ever more! May wretchedness, misery and death come to whoever wears it!" Andvari would have continued, but Loki and the treasure were already gone.

When Odin and Hoenir saw Loki returning with the enormous hoard of gold, they were mightily relieved. Eagerly, King Hreidmar and his sons watched as the three gods stuffed the otter skin until it was almost bursting, and carefully covered it, bit by bit. At last, all the gold was used up and the gods were done – or so they thought.

"Not so fast!" cried Hreidmar. "There is one hair on the otter's nose still showing. Either give up more gold or give up your lives!"

Luckily, Loki remembered Andvari's ring. "Take this with my pleasure," he smirked, throwing the band of bad luck onto the pile. And the gods gladly left the dwarves admiring their newfound wealth.

This is only the start of the curse of the ring. It continued to pass from hand to hand, bringing sorrow, wretchedness, misery and death to whoever wore it – just as Andvari had desired.

The Two Sisters

By Flora Annie Steel

ONCE UPON A TIME there were two sisters who were as like each other as two peas in a pod, but one was good, and the other was bad-tempered. Now their father had no work for them, so the girls began to think of going to be servants somewhere else.

"I will go first and see what I can make of it," said the younger sister, ever so cheerfully, "then you, sis, can follow if I have good luck."

So she packed up a bundle, said goodbye, and started to find a place, but no one in the town wanted a girl, so she went farther afield into the country. And as she journeyed she came upon an oven. In the oven, a lot of loaves were baking.

Now as she passed, the loaves cried out with one voice, "Little girl! Little girl! Take us out! Take us out! Please take us out! We have been baking for seven years, and no one has come to take us out. Do take us out or we shall soon be burnt! Seven years!"

Then, being a kind, obliging little girl, she stopped, put down her bundle, took out the bread from the oven, and went on her way saying, "You will be more comfortable now."

After a time she came to a cow lowing beside an empty pail, and the cow said to her, "Little girl! Little girl! Milk me! Milk me! Please milk me! Seven years have I been waiting, but no one has come to milk me! Seven years!"

So the kind girl stopped, put down her bundle, milked the cow into the pail, and went on her way saying, "Now you will be more comfortable."

By and by she came to an apple tree so laden with fruit that its branches were nigh to break, and the apple tree called to her:

"Little girl! Little girl! Shake my branches. Please shake my branches. The fruit is so heavy I can't stand straight!"

Then the kind girl stopped, put down her bundle,

and shook the branches so that the apples fell off, and the tree could stand straight. Then she went on her way saying, "You will be more comfortable now."

So she journeyed on till she came to a house where an old witch lived. Now this witch wanted a maid, and promised good wages. Therefore the girl agreed to stop with her and try how she liked service. She had to sweep the floor, keep the house clean and tidy, the fire bright and cheery. But there was one thing the witch said she must never do, and that was look up the chimney.

"If you do," said the witch, "something will fall down on you, and you will come to a bad end."

Well, the girl swept and dusted and made up the fire, but never a penny of wages did she see. Now the girl wanted to go home as she did not like witch service, for the witch used to have boiled babies for supper and bury the bones under some stones in the garden. But she did not like to go home penniless, so she stayed on, sweeping, and dusting and doing her work, just as if she was pleased.

Then one day, as she was sweeping up the hearth, down tumbled some soot, and, without remembering she was forbidden to look up the chimney, she looked up to see where the soot came from. And, lo and behold – a big bag of gold fell plump into her lap.

Now the witch happened to be out on one of her witch errands, so the girl thought it a fine opportunity to be off home.

So she kilted up her petticoats and started to run home but she had only gone a little way when she heard the witch coming after her on her broomstick. Now the apple tree she had helped to stand straight happened to be quite close, so she ran to it and cried,

"Apple tree! Apple tree, hide me
So the old witch can't find me,
For if she does she'll pick my bones,
And bury me under the garden stones."

Then the apple tree said, "Of course I will. You helped me to stand straight, and one good turn deserves another."

So the apple tree hid her finely in its green branches, and when the witch flew past saying,

"O Tree of mine! Tree of mine!
Have you seen my naughty little maid
With a willy willy wag and a great big bag,
She's stolen my money – all I had?"

The apple tree answered:

"No, Mother dear,
 Not for seven year!"

So the witch flew on the wrong way, and the girl got down, thanked the tree politely, and started again. But just as she got to where the cow was standing beside the pail, she heard the witch coming again, so she ran to the cow and cried,

"Cow! Cow, please hide me
 So the witch can't find me,
 If she does she'll pick my bones,
 And bury me under the garden stones!"

"Certainly I will," answered the cow. "Didn't you milk me and make me comfortable? Hide yourself behind me and you'll be quite safe."
 And when the witch flew by and called to the cow,

"O Cow of mine! Cow of mine!
 Have you seen my naughty little maid
 With a willy willy wag and a great big bag,
 Who stole my money – all I had?"

The cow just said politely:

"No, Mother dear,
 Not for seven year!"

Then the old witch went on in the wrong direction, and the girl started fresh on her way home, but just as

she got to where the oven stood, she heard that horrid old witch coming behind her again, so she ran as fast as she could to the oven and cried,
    "O Oven! Oven! hide me
    So as the witch can't find me,
    For if she does she'll pick my bones,
    And bury them under the garden stones."

Then the oven said, "I am afraid there is no room for you, as another batch of bread is baking, but there is the baker – ask him."

So she asked the baker, and he said, "Of course I will. You saved my last batch from being burnt, so run into the bakehouse, you will be quite safe there, and I will settle the witch for you."

So she hid in the bakehouse, only just in time, for there was the old witch calling angrily,

"O Man of mine! Man of mine!
 Have you seen my naughty little maid
 With a willy willy wag and a great big bag,
 Who's stole my money – all I had?"

Then the baker replied, "Look in the oven. She may be there."

And the witch alighted from her broomstick and peered into the oven, but she could see no one.

"Creep in and look in the farthest corner," said the baker slyly, and the witch crept in. Bang! He shut the door in her face, and there she was roasting. And when she came out with the bread she was all crisp and brown, and had to go home as best she could and put cold cream all over her!

But the kind, obliging little girl got safe home with her bag of money.

Now the ill-tempered elder sister was very jealous of this good luck, and determined to get a bag of gold for herself. So she in her turn packed up a bundle and started to seek service by the same road. But when she came to the oven, and the loaves begged her to take them out because they had been baking seven years and were nigh to burning, she tossed her head and said, "A likely story indeed, that I should burn my fingers to save your crusts. No, thank you!"

And with that she went on till she came across the cow standing waiting to be milked beside the pail. But when the cow said, "Little girl! Little girl! Milk me! Please milk me, I've waited seven years to be milked."

She only laughed and replied, "You may wait another seven years for all I care. I'm not your dairymaid!"

And with that she went on till she came to the apple tree, all overburdened by its fruit. But when it begged her to shake its branches, she only giggled, and plucking one ripe apple, said, "One is enough for me, you can keep the rest yourself." And with that she went on munching the apple, till she came to the witch's house.

Now the witch, though she had got over being crisp and brown from the oven, was dreadfully angry with all little maids, and made up her mind this one should not trick her. So for a long time she never went out of the house, thus the ill-tempered sister never had a chance of looking up the chimney, as she had meant to do at once. And she had to dust and clean and brush and sweep ever so hard, until she was quite tired out.

But one day, when the witch went into the garden to bury her bones, she seized the moment, looked up the chimney, and, sure enough, a bag of gold fell plump into her lap!

Well! She was off with it in a moment, and ran and ran till she came to the apple tree, when she heard the witch behind her. So she cried as her sister had done,

"Apple tree! Apple tree, hide me
  So the old witch can't find me,
  For if she does she'll break my bones,
  Or bury me under the garden stones."

But the apple tree said, "No room here! I've too many apples." So she had to run on, and when the witch on her broomstick came flying by and called,

"O Tree of mine! Tree of mine!
 Have you seen a naughty little maid
 With a willy willy wag and a great big bag,
 Who's stolen my money – all I had?"

The apple tree replied, "Yes, Mother dear, she's gone down there."

Then the witch went after her, caught her, gave her a thorough good beating, took the bag of money away from her, and sent her home without a penny payment for all her dusting, sweeping, brushing and cleaning.